Sunny

Rishelle.

Nick

ELMO

LIZ

EMILY RODDA'S
RAVEN HILL MYSTERIES

CASE #4: DEEP SECRETS

**Be on the lookout for all of
Emily Rodda's Raven Hill Mysteries:**

EMILY RODDA'S
RAVEN HILL MYSTERIES

CASE #4: DEEP SECRETS

Emily Rodda and Robert Sexton

APPLE SERIES

SCHOLASTIC INC.

New York   Toronto   London   Auckland   Sydney
Mexico City   New Delhi   Hong Kong   Buenos Aires

No part of this publication may be reproduced, stored in a retrieval system, or transmitted in any form or by any means, electronic, mechanical, photocopying, recording, or otherwise, without written permission of the publisher. For information regarding permission, write to Permissions Department, Scholastic Australia, P.O. Box 579, Lindfield, New South Wales, Australia 2070.

ISBN 0-439-78249-X

Series concept copyright © 1994 by Emily Rodda
Text copyright © 1994 by Scholastic Australia

All rights reserved. Published by Scholastic Inc., 557 Broadway, New York, NY 10012, by arrangement with Scholastic Press, an imprint of Scholastic Australia.

SCHOLASTIC, APPLE PAPERBACKS, and associated logos are trademarks and/or registered trademarks of Scholastic Inc.

12 11 10 9 8 7 6 5 4 3 2 1   6 7 8 9 10 11/0

Printed in the U.S.A.
First American edition, March 2006

Contents

1

The letter

No matter how hard we try to organize part-time work for Help-for-Hire Inc., our gang's job agency, we always seem to miss out during school vacation times. And spring break was looking like yet another vacation where we'd have no money-earning work to do.

It was Thursday afternoon, and school had just ended.

The gang — Liz Free, Tom Moysten, Richelle Brinkley, Nick Kontellis, and Sunny Chan — was at my house, waiting for my dad to turn up and pay us.

I was there, too, of course. My name's Elmo Zimmer. Together, the six of us make up Help-for-Hire Inc.

On Thursday mornings before school, we deliver the *Pen* — the local paper — around Raven Hill. Dad owns the *Pen*, and he usually pays us as soon as we get back to the office. But this morning, he was out when we arrived.

We'd been wanting to have a meeting about the lack of work, but in fact, we hadn't talked too much about that. We'd started watching this game show on TV and gotten sucked in. Now we were keeping score to see who got the most points.

"We'd better find a job soon," said Tom gloomily. "Or we'll get stuck with cleaning up our rooms again."

"Shush!" ordered Richelle. "The last question's coming up."

She was really interested because she had a good chance of winning.

Tom, who's only good at questions about art and food, was last. Nick, who thinks he's the smartest, was running second last. Sunny was fourth, Liz was third, and Richelle and I were tied for the top score.

I was doing well because I read a lot and keep up with the news, due to my job at the *Pen*. Richelle was doing well because so many of the questions were about film stars, ads, and TV shows. She loves all that stuff.

We stopped talking and listened to the question. The host smiled widely, showing all his teeth, and talked at the same time.

"What is Saint Elmo's fire?" he said.

Everyone looked blank, then stared at me. I shrugged.

"Don't you know?" drawled Nick.

"No," I said. "I'm named Elmo because my grandad was named Elmo, and he named my dad Elmo. That's it."

The TV contestants didn't know, either. The buzzer sounded.

"Saint Elmo's fire," said the TV man, still smiling, "is a luminous glow sometimes seen around high, projecting objects such as ships' masts and church spires during thunderstorms, snowstorms, and dust storms. Saint Elmo is the patron saint of sailors, and Saint Elmo's fire is said to be a sign of his protection."

"I was just about to say that," said Tom.

Sure.

"I won!" beamed Richelle. "And Elmo," she added.

"Crazy trick questions," Nick sneered. You wouldn't call him a bad loser, exactly. You'd call him a terrible loser.

Just at that moment, Dad came in. He was holding a piece of paper.

"Elmo," he said. "Guess what I've got."

"Our money?" asked Tom hopefully.

Dad nodded absentmindedly. "Oh, yes," he said, as if it didn't matter at all. "But, Elmo, I just received a letter from your great-aunt Vivien."

"Yeah? What about?" I said. It might seem strange that I was interested in a letter from my grandfather's sister. But my great-aunt Vivien wasn't exactly a big letter writer.

"Aunt Vivien — I can't believe it," Dad was saying to the others. "For all I knew she was dead. She lives in this huge old house way out in the sticks. It must be the third letter in thirty years."

"Dad, what does she want?" I asked, for the second time.

"You might not believe this," Dad said with a laugh. "But she wants Help-for-Hire to come and work for her. For money. And all expenses paid."

"What?" Now I was really astounded. Great-aunt Vivien and my grandfather hadn't liked each other much. Grandad used to say his sister was certifiably nuts and unworthy of the Zimmer name. She'd severed all ties with our side of the family. I'd never even met her.

"You won't want to do it, of course —" Dad began. Then he broke off in surprise because the gang was cheering, drowning him out.

3

"Saved!" chortled Tom. "Money!"

"A big, luxurious house," sighed Richelle.

"A vacation in the country for free!" grinned Liz.

"It won't be much of a vacation if I know Aunt Vivien," said Dad grimly.

That quieted them down.

"Ah . . . what do you mean, exactly, Zim?" asked Nick cautiously.

Dad ran his fingers through his hair in that way he does when he's stressed out.

"Well, I don't want to alarm you," he said — though I could see that he did, really. "But from what I remember of the old girl she wouldn't know a hard day's work if she fell over it. She's spent her whole life just traveling around the world and having fun."

"What's so bad about that?" asked Richelle, bewildered.

Dad shrugged. "Nothing so bad, I suppose," he admitted. "But what I mean is that she's never done a thing for anyone else in her life. She's never worked. She's just spent money. Stayed in expensive hotels, bought expensive clothes, and enjoyed herself."

Richelle went on looking blank. As far as she was concerned, this way of life sounded perfect.

Dad gave up trying to explain and went straight to the point.

"I think she's probably just asking you because . . . well, because it suits her. She thinks she's getting you cheap."

"Everyone gets us cheap," muttered Nick bitterly. He's always complaining our rates are too low. But, as Liz always says, no one'd be able to hire us to do odd jobs if we charged too much. Most people around Raven Hill couldn't afford it.

We looked at each other.

4

"Well, what do you think?" I asked.

"I'd like to go," Liz said. "I'd love a few days out of the city."

Sunny nodded. "We can go for long walks in our free time," she said.

Richelle shuddered. That was the last thing she had on her mind. But . . .

"I'd like some time in a really lovely house," she said. "Those old country mansions can be fabulous."

"I could do some sketching. And think of the meals," Tom put in. "Big country breakfasts, morning snack time with biscuits and jam, enormous country lunches, afternoon snack time with chocolate-chip cookies and homemade lemonade. Dinners with . . ."

"I don't know," said Nick, breaking in before Tom actually started drooling. "Stuck way out there for days. Paid peanuts."

"We don't all have to go," said Liz in an offhand sort of way. "You could stay home, Nick. We'll just split the peanuts five ways instead of six."

Liz is smart. If you ever want to change Nick's mind, talk about money.

"Still . . . all expenses paid," he said thoughtfully. "It's probably worth it. I guess."

"So it's on?" asked Tom eagerly.

They hadn't asked me what I thought. They were just assuming I was in. After all, Vivien was *my* great-aunt. But I really didn't want to go.

"I don't know Aunt Vivien at all, you know," I told them. "And even Dad has only met her a few times. The job might be a complete disaster."

5

"We won't blame you, Elmo," said Liz. "And anyway, everything'll be fine."

"Sure. What can go wrong?" shrugged Tom.

That should have made us all stop and think. Anytime anyone's ever said that in the past, we've found ourselves up to our necks in trouble.

But no one said anything. The others were all too busy with their own private dreams about how good the new job was going to be. And I was too busy being nervous because Aunt Vivien was my aunt, and the job had come to us through Dad. Whatever they said, everyone would blame me if they didn't enjoy themselves.

"Dad, she did actually ask for the whole gang, didn't she?" I said. "I mean, how would she know Help-for-Hire even exists?"

"She's been reading about you in the *Pen*, apparently," Dad mumbled. "Following the stories about your crime-busting activities. Not that she's interested in that, of course. It's the job agency she's after."

I raised my eyebrows in surprise. "How would Aunt Vivien see the *Pen*?"

"The *Pen*'s sent to her every week," Dad said, looking a bit embarrassed. "I organized that after I took over the paper. After your grandfather died."

"I didn't know that!" I exclaimed.

"I thought — well, at the time I thought it might be nice to try to keep in touch," Dad muttered. "These family feuds are stupid. But she never wrote thanking me or anything. As far as I knew, she was throwing the papers straight into the trash. But I guess she wasn't."

"Of course she wasn't." Soft-hearted Liz beamed. "That's so nice. After all this time, the dear old lady wants to get to know Elmo. That's why she's asked us to work for her, for sure. It's all just an excuse to see him."

"She's never shown any interest before," said Dad doubtfully. "We sent her a photograph when he was a baby, but . . ."

"I bet she thought he was so cute and cuddly," Tom teased.

Richelle giggled, and I felt myself blushing.

"Anyway, that decides it for sure," Liz announced. "We'll definitely go."

The others nodded.

Dad ran his fingers through his hair again. "Well, it's your funeral," he sighed. "You'll have to check it out with your parents. Give us a call tonight, to confirm. Then I'll write to Vivien and set it up. You'll go by train. How about you plan to leave right after the next *Pen* delivery?"

"But that's a whole week away!" exclaimed Liz. "Can't we make it sooner?"

Dad shook his head. "Not really," he said. "It all has to be organized by letter. There's no phone or e-mail at Mistfall."

"Not even a *phone?*" squeaked Richelle in horror.

"Mistfall!" breathed Liz at the same moment. "What a great name."

"What's great about it? It sounds sort of . . . damp," quavered Richelle. She touched her long, wavy fair hair in a worried sort of way. A damp place with no phone! Richelle was starting to wish she hadn't agreed to this job so easily.

And I was wishing I hadn't agreed at all.

2

Destination: nowhere

Dad wrote to Aunt Vivien the next day, and the reply came back early the following week. Aunt Vivien was looking forward to seeing us, especially me. She'd expect us to arrive by train on Friday.

There was no discussion about which train. It turned out there was only one. And there wasn't any discussion about how long we'd stay, either. There was no train back to the city from Kneebone, Aunt Vivien said, till Monday morning.

"*Kneebone?*" snorted Nick, when he heard this. "I don't *believe* there's a place called Kneebone!"

"There is," I said. "Aunt Vivien's address is 'Mistfall via Kneebone.' I saw it on her letter."

"Well, whoever heard of a train station where the trains only stop twice a week!" exclaimed Richelle.

I shrugged. "Want to change your minds?" I asked hopefully.

"No!" said Liz. "We're going to have our vacation in the country, and you're going to have that reunion with your great-aunt if it kills me, Elmo Zimmer."

"It might," I said darkly.

"Mistfall via Kneebone," murmured Tom. "Sounds like a good place to die."

He thought he was joking.

❈

On Friday morning, we were on our way. We'd already changed trains once, and we still had hours of travel stretching in front of us. No one was in a particularly good mood.

"I was thinking, you know," Liz said, staring out the window. "Aunt Vivien will have to send two cars to pick us up. Otherwise, we won't all fit in."

"It'll probably be a cattle truck," said Tom drearily.

"Sure, sure." Nick jeered. "They'll send a car for us and a cattle truck for you, Moysten."

"At least I'll be in better company than I'm in now."

"Can't you two ever stop?" cried Liz.

I didn't say anything. I was too busy thinking. I wasn't looking forward to seeing Aunt Vivien.

Grandad hadn't liked her. He'd always said she was certifiably nuts, as he put it. I imagined some embarrassing, vain, fussy old woman wearing fancy clothes who laughed all the time. She'd probably bore everyone silly with stories about her travels. She'd probably want to kiss me and leave red lipstick all over my face.

Richelle was sulking. It had started because Nick had promised to bring his cell phone with him, and then at the last minute had left it at home.

9

"I couldn't help it, Richelle," he'd told her. "It's not working properly. It's got to be fixed."

"You should have checked it out last week!" she'd pouted. "Now we're going to be stuck out in the middle of nowhere without a phone."

"Come on, Richelle," Liz said. "Even *you* can live without a phone for a couple of days."

"Yeah," said Tom. "It'll give your ear a chance to get back to normal."

Her eyes widened. "What do you mean?"

"Oh, you know," he said casually. "The way your right ear's sort of flattened out and gotten bigger than the other one? That's because of the phone, isn't it?"

Richelle's hand flew to her right ear, and she turned crimson.

Tom turned to Nick. "You've noticed Richelle's ear, haven't you, Nick?"

Nick nodded seriously. "Oh, yeah," he said. "But I didn't want to say anything."

By now, Richelle had one hand on her ear, and one over her mouth, and her eyes looked as though they were going to fall out of her head.

"Richelle, it's all right," said Liz, half-laughing, half-angry with Tom and Nick.

"There's nothing wrong with your ear, Richelle," sighed Sunny. "They're just playing around."

But it took a while for Richelle to calm down. And when she finally did, she went into a long, injured silence that lasted for practically the whole trip.

By the time another hour had passed, Nick, Liz, Richelle, and Tom were asleep, rocking with the movement of the train. Sunny was still awake, but she was just staring out the window as if she was hypnotized.

There was practically no one left in our car except these two big, mean-looking guys wearing dark suits and sunglasses. They kept looking at us, and grinning at one another, as though there was something about us they found funny.

They worried me.

I wondered where they were going. As far as I could tell, they were going nowhere. The same as us.

Destination: Kneebone. Code name for nowhere. A tiny dot on the map with a whole lot of space around it. One of lots of other tiny dots, linked only by the train line and the road that ran alongside it.

Maybe the men were going to another one of the dots. To rob a bank, maybe. Or to set up shop as funeral directors. Or they could be railway detectives who rode the train all day and night, looking for people who hadn't paid their fares, or put their feet on the seats.

Anyway, I wished they'd move into another car. But even if they did, they wouldn't be very far away. There were only two cars for people in the whole train. The rest of the train was made up of freight cars.

I looked out the window and wished I'd come down with chicken pox or tonsilitis. Even an earache. Anything to get out of this.

But there was no way out. To Kneebone we were going, whether I liked it or not. So I decided to get out of the situation the only way I could. I closed my eyes like the others, and dozed.

I woke up when the train pulled into this tiny little station. "Kneebone!" called the guard, walking through the carriage and roaring as though it was full of people. "Kneebone!"

We gathered up our stuff and climbed out of the train. Flies descended on us happily.

"Good luck!" the guard said, and winked at me.

Then he stood back.

The two men in suits were getting out, too.

There was no one to meet us. Not that we could see, anyway.

We stood around on the station platform for a while, just waiting. But still no one appeared on the road outside. No minibus. No fleet of cars. No cattle truck.

Tom found a small poster lying on the platform. It was advertising a wrestling match. Here in the Kneebone Town Hall on Saturday night.

"Who says this place isn't jumping?" he grinned.

One of the wrestlers was wearing a Roman gladiator's costume. He even had a wreath of leaves around his head. He was called "The Killer." The other was more like the evil monster in a late-night movie. He was "The Freak." They were both wearing face paint, and were glaring at one another, with clenched fists.

Tom got out his pen and, in his words, gave the wrestlers "a bit of life."

He gave them bow ties, earrings, nose rings, little curved horns, striped socks, and flower tattoos on their chests.

"How's that?" he said, when he'd finished.

"Much better," said Liz. But I noticed that she glanced up the tiny platform and back again in a worried sort of way. She was wondering what we were going to do if no one turned up for us.

Richelle didn't care about worrying anyone.

"Nick Kontellis," she said sternly. "If you'd only said your cell phone wasn't working, I finally could have convinced my dad to get me one. Now look at the mess we're in. We can't even call a taxi."

"A taxi?" Nick snorted. "Where do you think you are, Richelle? There are no taxis here."

I left Richelle and Nick arguing about the phone we didn't have, and went to find someone who could help us.

There was a sort of shed in the center of the platform. I knocked at the door.

After a while, a man came out and stared at me. He was an old guy who needed a shave and a set of teeth. He had on a railroad hat and coat so I guessed he worked there.

"Excuse me," I said. "Somebody was coming to meet us."

"I haven't seen no one," he said.

"Someone from Mistfall." I thought the name might mean something to him. I pointed in the direction I thought the cars or whatever might come from. "It's that way, isn't it?"

He pushed his cap back on his head. A few bits of white hair poked out from under the peak.

"Mistfall? Now lemme see . . ."

I could tell he'd take all day to think about it.

"It's okay. Thanks, anyway." I nodded for the gang to follow me and headed for the exit.

"Mistfall," the old man called out behind us. "Yeah. Mistfall's about six miles up the road. Dunno why you wanna go there."

"My great-aunt lives there," I said.

"That right?" he said. He munched his bare gums together.

We didn't want to stand there talking to the guy so we kept moving. Out of the station, onto the road.

The guys in suits had disappeared. I wondered where they'd gone.

The road was just a dirt track. And Kneebone itself seemed to consist entirely of a general store, a gas station, a tiny fire station, a diner, three houses, and a rickety wooden building with a corrugated iron roof and TOWN HALL painted over its door.

My heart leaped as I saw a cloud of dust heading down the road toward us.

"There you are," said Liz brightly. "Our ride."

We picked up our bags and waited.

3

Death Valley

The dustball turned into a big, black car with darkened windows. It swung off the road and stopped, just in front of us. We started walking toward it.

Then, suddenly, the two big guys in suits wandered out of the diner. Casually, they crossed the road, threw their bags into the car, and got into the backseat.

I couldn't see the driver. Nor could I see the men once they were inside. I could see only our grotesque reflections in the one-way glass. We all had big heads, very big noses, and tiny little bodies.

And very depressed expressions.

The car roared away, leaving us standing in a cloud of dust.

"Buses usually meet the trains at country stations," Tom said, after a moment. "So we'll just wait here till a bus comes, okay?"

"Dream on, Moysten," Nick drawled. "There's not going to be a bus."

"There are always buses in the country," Tom said. "Eventually. I know these things, Kontellis."

The toothless railroad guy toddled up to us.

"No good standin' there," he said.

"We're waiting for a bus," said Tom politely.

The man laughed, showing all his gums. "Be a long wait," he said. "Isn't due till Monday morning."

"Thanks," Nick said. He glared at Tom, then looked around scornfully. "What a place!" he hissed.

"Nothing wrong with this place. City kids. Got no sense, have ya?" the toothless guy mumbled as he turned away.

Nick was in his worst aggro mood. He followed the old man.

"What do you mean by that?"

"Just what I said. Shoulda found out where you was going before ya left home, shouldn't ya?"

Liz stepped between them. "I'm sorry," she said. "It's just that we've come all this way, and we're a bit tired."

"Well, little lady, you're gonna be a lot more tired, time you get to Mistfall," croaked the toothless man.

Liz tried to smile. "How far is it?" she asked.

"Six miles, about," said the man, with a satisfied smile. "That way." He pointed to the left, down a dirt road that stretched off into the distance like Death Valley.

"OK," Liz said, firmly leading Nick away. "Thank you. We'd better get started, then."

Oh, no, I thought. *Oh, please, let me still be dreaming.*

But I wasn't dreaming. I was in Kneebone. And so was everyone else. This was hideous reality.

"Look at yer," the old man called after us as we trailed away. "Half of yer's not dressed for a six-mile hike."

I glanced back at him. He grinned widely and pointed at Richelle. "By the look of them shoes, you'll be carrying her before you get half way," he yelled.

With a cackle of laughter, he went back to the station.

And we started walking.

Six hot, dusty, deadly miles to Mistfall.

"What's six miles in city blocks?" Richelle asked.

"Dozens," said Sunny, who was already on her way. "Come on, guys, or we'll never get there."

Richelle looked as if she was going to die. She swatted helplessly at some flies.

"Come on!" Sunny called as she jogged on the spot about fifty feet up the road. "Six miles is nothing."

But we'd only been walking ten minutes before I'd decided that anything would be better than this. It would be nice to be home, digging the moldy vegetables out of the fridge crisper. It would be heavenly to be scraping the congealed fat out of the backyard grill.

My bag was getting heavier by the second. Richelle screamed every time a fly settled on her face. She made me edgy.

My sneakers had gotten thin underneath. I could feel every stone I walked on. I should have accepted the offer of a new pair when Dad was feeling generous a couple of weeks ago. But my old ones felt so comfortable and lived-in then. Now I might as well have taken them off for all the good they were doing.

Nick made up his mind the walk wasn't going to beat him. He strode ahead with Sunny and Liz, leaving Tom, Richelle, and me behind.

As we trudged along, a few cars and a pickup truck passed by. A couple of the drivers stared at us. But no one stopped.

"I thought people were supposed to be friendly in the country," complained Richelle.

"We'd be stupid to take a ride from a stranger, anyway," said Liz. "You can get killed that way."

"I'm practically dead now," sniffed Richelle.

A shiny green SUV roared by. We were covered in its dust and had to stop, coughing and spluttering.

But do you think the driver cared? No way. He sat there, hiding behind his sunglasses, pretending not to see us. His ponytail was flying in the wind as he roared past. He had the radio blaring. He looked as if he didn't have a worry in the world. And he was drinking a can of Coke.

We would have killed for that can of Coke.

"Can you *believe* he could do that?" Richelle screeched.

But in spite of him, and Richelle's screams, and the stones, we finally reached a little intersection where a faded sign said MISTFALL 2 MILES. Liz, Sunny, and Nick were sitting on a rock waiting for us.

"Richelle," Sunny called. "See? You did it. Just shows what you can do if you try."

Richelle stared at her but said nothing. That was worse than if she'd shouted at the top of her voice.

Just then, a cloud of dust appeared over the brow of a hill ahead of us. We all stood back as the car passed. We didn't want another dust bath.

It was the same black monster that had picked up the guys

in the suits. But it seemed to be empty of passengers now. It had dropped off the guys and was heading back to base.

It wasn't any help. But at least it gave us something to talk about, besides our sore feet and the flies.

"Who do you think those guys were?" Sunny asked.

"Probably a couple of spies," Nick said.

"Don't be stupid, Nick," Richelle said. "There's nothing out here to spy on."

Liz sighed. "Whoever they are, and whatever they're doing, I'll bet they're having a better time than us."

And no one was arguing with her about that.

4

Mistfall

As we got closer to Mistfall, Sunny ran on ahead of us – up a hill and over the other side. A few minutes later, she came jogging back.

"I wish she'd stop doing that," groaned Tom. "It makes me even more exhausted just looking at her."

"Hey, guys," Sunny shouted. "It's just over the hill. You can see it. Just a few more minutes. Come on!"

On the train I'd been dreading seeing Aunt Vivien. But now, after walking through Death Valley for what seemed like six thousand miles instead of six, I couldn't wait.

Everyone else must have felt the same way. They all started walking faster. Even Richelle.

We talked about what we were going to do when we arrived.

Richelle wanted a long, hot shower. All Nick and Liz cared about was a long, cool drink. Tom wanted food. Lots of food. I wanted two new feet. Sunny probably wanted to go back to the railroad station and start running all over again.

Full of new energy, we powered up that hill. And just as Sunny had promised, we were soon stumbling down the other side, with our eyes fixed on the big house in the valley.

It wasn't exactly what anyone had expected.

"Oh, what a marvelous old place," said Liz. But she didn't sound as enthusiastic as usual.

We slowed down a bit, staring at what was going to be our home for the next couple of days.

One thing was for sure. It was a big house. A very big house. It was made of big blocks of gray stone.

One end of the building looked a bit like one of those forts you see in films about Europe in the Middle Ages. It had a tower with slitted windows. You could just imagine archers shooting at the enemy from there. The other end of the house was like a church with a tall steeple.

Sticking up from the tower and the steeple were long thin lightning rods.

"It looks half like a castle and half like a pretend church," said Richelle. "It's weird."

"It's a monstrosity," said Nick. "Who'd build a house like that?"

"Dr. Frankenstein," Tom said.

"And you." Richelle snapped at him. "You like all that weirdo stuff."

"Yeah," Tom grinned, feasting his eyes on the weird old place. "Look at the turrets and spires and stuff. And the stained-glass windows. Isn't it great?"

Nick sneered.

We finally reached the gate at the bottom of the hill. It was high, with iron railings. MISTFALL was engraved on a dull brass plate screwed on to one side. We stood looking up the weedy drive. The door was at the tower end of the house, and so huge that three of us could have walked through it side by side.

The garden was completely overgrown — just a mass of huge, spreading bushes and long grass, with lots of flowers growing wild everywhere, and bunches of seed pods rattling in the breeze. It reminded me of an old cemetery, except that the gravestones were missing.

The whole place was definitely weird, and very spooky-looking. And it was the middle of the day.

I could imagine it in the full moon, with long shadows making the whole scene even more scary. Like houses they have in movies where you've got witches and vampires and rats and blood dripping from the ceiling.

We backed away from the gate.

"This place gives me the creeps," Richelle whispered.

"Why are you whispering?" Tom whispered.

"Oh, come on," Liz said loudly. "Let's go in."

"Yes," said Sunny, putting her hand through the big iron gate railings. "We won't do any good standing here."

The gate creaked open. Little bits of rusty iron fell off it as it swung back, away from us.

"Well, we made it," I said, trying to sound cheerful.

No one answered me as we walked quickly up the drive.

There was a big, white Rolls Royce car parked in a garage behind the house. The garage doors were open, and we could see it clearly, just sitting there.

"We could have all fit into that," said Richelle crossly. "And I've always wanted to ride in a Rolls."

No one answered her, either.

We'd almost reached the house when the big front door swung open. A frowning, black-haired, thin-lipped woman emerged from the dimness and stood staring at us.

I opened my mouth to say something, but the words died in my throat as she abruptly turned back into the house and spoke to someone standing behind her. The next moment a bony-faced man with a thin black mustache appeared beside her.

Who's that? I thought, confused. Dad said Aunt Vivien wasn't married.

"Hey, you kids! Clear off!" the man shouted.

We stopped dead. Everyone looked at me. I could feel my face getting red. I shuffled forward a couple of steps.

"It's me, Aunt Vivien," I said to the woman, trying to smile. "Elmo."

The woman gaped at me. "*Who?*" she demanded.

My stomach was tying itself into knots. This was terrible! Could Aunt Vivien possibly have forgotten about inviting us? And why didn't she recognize me? She'd seen my picture in the *Pen*.

I cleared my throat. "You know," I said. "Elmo. Your nephew. Your . . . um . . . grand-nephew. Come for the weekend. To work. Dad wrote to you. Remember?"

A strange expression crossed the woman's face. She seemed to be thinking quickly. Then she bared her teeth in what was probably supposed to be a smile.

"Oh. Yes. It had slipped my mind you were coming today,"

she said. "But I'm afraid it's not very convenient. Maybe another weekend. You'd better run along home now."

She started to close the door.

I heard the gang groaning softly behind me.

"But-but, Aunt Vivien, it was all organized. You wrote to Dad —" I shouted in desperation. "He wrote back to you. He told you we were coming. And we can't go home. There's no train."

The woman hesitated. She muttered something I couldn't hear to the man beside her. He shook his head and muttered back, as if he was arguing with her. But finally she opened the door wide again and beckoned impatiently.

"You'd better come in, then," she snapped.

We stumbled up the steps. Not that I wanted to. And I'm sure the rest of the gang was feeling exactly like I was. But at that moment we didn't have any choice.

The woman watched us silently as we crowded inside. Now that I was closer to her, I could see that she was much younger than she'd seemed at a distance. And very much younger than Aunt Vivien could possibly be.

My surprise must have shown in my face, because again she gave that awful, fake smile. Her thin lips were covered with very dark red lipstick, and her eyebrows were as thin as pencil lines.

"What a mix-up," she murmured. "I can't imagine what you'll think of us."

"You're not my Aunt Vivien, are you?" I blurted out.

She raised her eyebrows. "Of course I'm not, dear," she said. "I'm Miss Zimmer's housekeeper, Mrs. Everedd. And this is my husband, who manages the farm." She gestured at the bony-faced man hovering behind her. He nodded briefly at me, uncomfortably fingering his thin mustache.

"Oh . . . er . . . I'm . . . er . . . sorry. It's just I haven't seen my great-aunt since . . . um . . . well, I've never met her, actually," I heard myself burbling.

I knew I was sounding like a complete idiot. I was so embarrassed I felt as though I was melting.

"That's quite all right," smiled the woman. "I understand. Unfortunately, Miss Zimmer hadn't told me you were expected. She's a bit forgetful these days. But never mind."

Great. No wonder we hadn't been met at the station. Aunt Vivien had completely forgotten we were even coming. I remembered Grandad's unflattering description of her. She must have gotten worse with age. What had I gotten the gang into?

"Where is she?" I asked, looking around.

For the first time, I noticed just how nice the house was inside. It was beautiful, really, with polished wood and thick rugs on the floor, and a clean, fresh smell. Not at all what you would have expected.

"Miss Zimmer hasn't been very well today. She's resting," the housekeeper said smoothly. "Why don't you go visit the kitchen and have something to eat? My husband will look after you. I'll go and see if Miss Zimmer's awake."

"Thank you, Mrs. . . . ?" I hesitated. I'd completely forgotten her name.

"Mrs. Everedd," she said. And again she smiled. A smile that was more like a snarl than anything else.

"Mrs. Never-dead, more like it," Tom breathed in my ear.

I smothered a hysterical snort of laughter. Mr. and Mrs. Never-dead. That would be right. As we followed the silent man to the kitchen, I decided that the Never-deads were the perfect ending to a perfect nightmare.

Little did I know that it was just the beginning.

5

Hello, Aunt Vivien

The kitchen was huge and bright, and paneled with honey-colored wood. There was a long table and a dresser stacked with colorful plates at one end.

The table stood in front of a big, wide window — nothing like the narrow windows you could see from the road. It faced out to the hillside behind the house.

The view was lovely. The hill was green and covered with trees. All sorts of birds flew around, and there were deer grazing in groups.

"Look at that!" breathed Liz, gazing out at the view with a dreamy look on her face.

"Look at *that!*" muttered Tom. He pointed. His eyes were bulging. Mr. Never-dead had opened a door to reveal a giant walk-in pantry stacked with food, and two tall fridges.

"Sit down," Mr. Never-dead called over his shoulder, foraging in the pantry.

We did. Suddenly, we were feeling a lot better. Cake, we were all picturing. Apple pie. Hot scones. Cold lemonade.

But, in the end, the man came out carrying a small packet of plain crackers, and a half-used bottle of orange soda. He put them on the table, then, sighing, went off to get glasses and a jug of water from the tap.

"Dig in," he said, slamming the glasses down.

He leaned against one of the cupboards and watched us.

We sat there nibbling crackers and pouring soda. We were all hungry and thirsty, and so we were grateful, in a way, for anything we got. But it was a bit of a letdown after all our greedy imaginings.

We were still sitting there about fifteen minutes later. We'd finished the crackers and the soda, but there didn't seem much point in moving. Then the sound of two pairs of footsteps in the next room made us all turn our heads.

"They're in here, Miss Zimmer," we heard Mrs. Never-dead saying.

The next moment, they were in the kitchen. Mrs. Never-dead was holding Aunt Vivien tightly by the arm. I decided the old lady must be frailer than I'd thought.

"Well, here they are," Mrs. Never-dead said loudly. She pointed to me. "There's Elmo, see?"

My first sight of Aunt Vivien gave me quite a shock. I hadn't expected her to be young, or very good-looking, or anything. But I hadn't expected her to be like she was, either.

She wasn't as wrinkled as I'd thought she'd be, but she was twice as ugly. I have to say that because it's true. She'd put on a lot of makeup to try to brighten herself up, but it didn't help. If anything, it made things worse. Her straight, stringy hair hung to her shoulders. She would have been tall if she hadn't stooped so much. But she did stoop.

And her clothes! They were incredibly depressing. I don't care much about clothes myself, but you didn't have to be Richelle to think Aunt Vivien was in a pretty bad state.

She wore a grungy skirt that went up and down at the hem, a checkered blouse, a ragged-looking cardigan, and a string of beads that fit so tightly around her neck that they looked like they were choking her.

She was also wearing thick woolen tights and sneakers. Very worn sneakers. Worse than mine!

But it wasn't just her face and clothes that startled me. It was the way she was.

I'd expected someone who was talkative, and confident — even if she *was* certifiably nuts. But in fact my aunt was the opposite. She seemed very, very nervous. Her eyes darted everywhere as Mrs. Never-dead led her forward. She sniffed, and dabbed at her nose with a crumpled tissue. And she didn't say a word — to me, or anyone else.

"It seems there's been a mistake, Elmo," said Mrs. Neverdead. "When Miss Zimmer got your father's letter, she thought he wrote 'next month,' not 'next week.' She wouldn't have agreed to the visit now — not in her present state of health."

"Oh, yes," Richelle said eagerly. "That's an easy mistake to make. We'll just go straight home." Her eyes sparkled at the thought of getting away.

"Miss Zimmer was going to suggest the same thing," said Mrs. Never-dead. She turned to Aunt Vivien. "Weren't you,

Miss Zimmer?" she asked loudly. And I could have sworn her hand tightened on the old woman's arm.

Aunt Vivien nodded and mumbled.

"First thing in the morning," said Mrs. Never-dead. "Seeing as you said there were no more trains today."

"There are no trains till Monday!" Liz exclaimed.

Mrs. Never-dead's face fell. Aunt Vivien sniffed uncomfortably, and dabbed her nose again.

"That's okay," Richelle said with her most winning smile. "I was thinking. We don't want to be any trouble by staying till Monday. Maybe Mr. Never — um, I mean, Mr. Everedd — could drive us. I saw a Rolls in the garage. We'd all fit into that."

Mrs. Never-dead glanced at her husband, and frowned. "Unfortunately, that's impossible," she snapped. "The Rolls needs repair. It can't be driven. There's no way in the world we can take you to the city."

You could see that she was telling the truth. She'd have loved to get rid of us. She hesitated. Just for a moment, she seemed at a loss as to what to do next.

I took the opportunity to speak to Aunt Vivien directly. I'm usually quite shy, but she seemed even more nervous than I was. And I found myself feeling quite worried about her.

"It's nice to meet you after all this time, Aunt Vivien," I said. "These are the other members of Help-for-Hire."

She sniffed anxiously. Her eyes widened.

"Sunny, Liz, Nick, Tom, and Richelle," I told her, speaking slowly and pointing at the gang one at a time. "You remember. You saw their pictures in the *Pen*, didn't you?"

She swallowed, nodded, and glanced nervously at Mrs. Never-dead. "Yes," she whispered.

"I think Miss Zimmer is getting overtired," said Mrs. Never-dead, raising her thin black eyebrows. She began ushering Aunt Vivien out of the room.

As she went, she looked back over her shoulder at her husband. "Take them out to the yard," she snapped at him. "They can clean it up. Later, they can clean out the Rolls garage. And the well."

He cleared his throat, as though he was going to argue with her again.

"They should be outside," she said firmly. "In the open air. Miss Zimmer tells me they're here to work. So they can work. The yard should keep them busy for a while."

She gave Aunt Vivien a little push, and propelled her out of sight.

Mr. Never-dead took us outside to clean up the yard. He handed us each a plastic bag.

"Pick up every scrap of paper you can see," he said.

So we started picking up papers. It was just like being on detention.

This was turning out to be the worst day of my life. And the others were griping about everything, which didn't help.

Tom kept complaining that he was still hungry.

Richelle and Nick — superior, never-get-anything-wrong Nick — were whispering about Aunt Vivien's clothes.

Liz and Sunny were embarrassed for me, because my aunt was so weird.

But I was puzzled and worried. Aunt Vivien might not be the cleverest and most beautiful woman in the world, but she was still my aunt. And I couldn't help remembering how nervous she'd seemed. And how tightly Mrs. Never-dead had gripped her arm.

There was something very strange going on.

6

Settling in

In spite of all our complaints, we stuck to the job. It was boring work, but it wasn't as if it was too difficult. And looking for garbage gave us a chance to see what the grounds around the house were like.

There were two garages. One for the Rolls, and a locked one, which Mr. Never-dead said was being used as a storeroom.

The Rolls garage looked as if it had been used as a storeroom, too. On every wall there were shelves from floor to ceiling stacked with boxes and papers and other junk.

There was a shed with a noisy generator in it chugging away making electricity for the house. Aunt Vivien had to make her own power.

Luckily, though, she was obviously connected to town water. The well hadn't been used for years.

Because, eventually, we found it, too. It was quite a long way from the house, in a sort of gully. It was just a very deep hole in the ground. There was no built-up wall around it like in pictures of Jack-and-Jill wells.

A heavy wooden lid was fitted over the top, to stop people

falling down by accident, we guessed. We moved the lid and dropped a stone down. It took a count of two before we heard it hit something that sounded tinny on the bottom.

"There's no water in it," exclaimed Sunny, in surprise.

"That's probably because it's clogged up with junk," I said.

"It's pretty deep," muttered Nick. "I'm not going down there."

"Me, neither," chorused Tom and Richelle.

Maybe we won't have to," said Liz hopefully. "Maybe it'll take us too long to do the other things. After all, we've only got today, and Saturday, and Sunday. . . ."

Her voice trailed off, and we all looked at each other. It sounded like an eternity.

In silence, we heaved the lid back onto the well, and went back to cleaning up.

○

When we thought we'd finished, we took the bags of paper to the back door and called out to Mrs. Never-dead.

"Good," she said, peering at us. "Now, get your bags. I'll show you your rooms and get you settled in."

"Oh, yes!" said Richelle, who'd been talking about having a shower ever since we got there.

"You'll be sleeping in the west wing," she said. "This way."

We grabbed our bags and followed her out of the kitchen along a passage to a big room. The room was roughly round, like the spire. There was a huge table in the middle with twelve chairs around it.

On one side of the room, there was a big, heavy door. The carved panels gleamed, the brass doorknob shone. I wondered where the door led to, and asked Mrs. Never-dead.

"The tower wing," she said. "That whole area is Miss Zimmer's private quarters. Nothing to do with you."

Stairs curved up from the other end of the room to an open level — a "mezzanine," Mrs. Never-dead called it. She led us up, walking stiffly.

You could look down from the mezzanine and see everything in the room below. Lots of doors led off it. And there were more stairs going up above us to another level. I imagined there would be more rooms up there.

"Girls on this level," Mrs. Never-dead said crisply. "Boys on the next one up."

She opened one of the doors, and we looked inside.

"What a nice room," Liz smiled.

The bedroom was narrow near the door and widened out at the outside wall. It was like a big slice of cake with the point cut off.

The other bedrooms were the same. I was thankful to see that they were very clean. There was no dust at all, and a faint smell of furniture polish. The beds were already made up with crisp sheets.

I was thankful, but it was odd. There hadn't been time for Mrs. Never-dead to prepare all these bedrooms. They must have been made up before.

That meant Aunt Vivien really *had* been expecting us. *She must just be really forgetful*, I thought.

Mrs. Never-dead hadn't stopped talking.

"You girls use the bathroom along there," she said, pointing. "There's another one for the boys on their floor."

So, at last, we all had hot showers and changed into clean clothes.

"Aaaah," said Richelle, when we met downstairs later. "Now I feel human again. Even if I did get hurried out of the shower." She glared at Sunny, who just grinned and shrugged.

It was still daylight. We'd thought we might go for a walk and see the deer. But Mrs. Never-dead told us it was time for dinner.

We sat around the kitchen table and ate. I think I can honestly say it was the worst meal I've ever eaten. Worse than summer camp. And that's saying something.

We picked at the food. A few fatty, warmed-up meat bits cut from the very last remains of a roast; soggy, gray-green, half-cold brussels sprouts; lumpy mashed potatoes with brown bits in them; and gravy that tasted like mud.

Even Tom wouldn't eat it.

"Two stars," said Nick, judging it like a hotel. "Great beds, hopeless food."

Liz glanced at me, worried that I'd be hurt because this was my aunt's house. But I wasn't, really. Aunt Vivien wasn't responsible for this. It was all Mrs. Never-dead. She didn't want us here. And she was going all out to make sure we didn't want to be here, either.

Just then, the woman herself came back into the kitchen.

"All right," she said, looking at our plates. "Obviously, you weren't very hungry. You'd better clean up, then."

"I've got room for dessert," said Tom hopefully.

"There's no dessert, I'm afraid," snapped Mrs. Never-dead. "You can stack the dishwasher now, and then you'd better go straight to bed. You've got a hard day ahead of you tomorrow."

"But it's so early!" Richelle protested.

"We all go to bed early here, dear." The woman smiled thinly.

"I'd like to say good night to Aunt Vivien," I said.

"Oh, she's in bed," said Mrs. Never-dead. "She won't feel like seeing anyone now."

And obviously, as far as she was concerned, that was the end of it.

7

Lights out

I was changing, getting ready for bed, listening to the rumbling of distant thunder, when everything went black. I rushed out of my room and found myself staring at Nick and Tom, who'd done exactly the same. From the floor below we could hear Richelle complaining and calling out to Liz.

"Must be a blackout," said Nick. "It's thundering."

"Wake up, Kontellis. This house doesn't have the power on, so there can't be a blackout," jeered Tom. "They've just turned off the generator."

Richelle's voice rose to a shriek. "Nothing works!" she squealed. "My room's pitch-black!"

"Sorry about that," Mrs. Never-dead's voice echoed from downstairs. "We've turned off the generator. The power won't be back on till six in the morning."

"I can't see anything!" complained Richelle.

"Just go to sleep!" yelled Mrs. Never-dead.

"Might as well," Nick grumbled. "Nothing else to do." But there was no way I could sleep. I lay there in the dark, wide awake, listening to the thunder and the old house creaking.

After about half an hour, I'd had enough. I got up and pulled on my jeans.

I crept out into the hallway and knocked softly on Tom's door. He was in the room next to mine.

"It's Elmo," I whispered. "Are you awake?"

"No. Are you?" he whispered back. There was a thud as his feet hit the floor, then his door opened and he came out. His hair was sticking up on end, but he was fully dressed except for his shoes.

"This place spooks me," he said. "And I'm starving to death. I've been just lying there listening to my stomach rumble in time with the thunder."

Nick must have heard our voices. He came out of his room as well. He hadn't changed for bed, either. But his hair was as smooth as ever. I've never understood how Nick stays so neat.

"I think we should talk," I said in a low voice. "I think something's going on around here."

We crept down to the girls' level. We could hear low voices coming from Liz's room. We knocked and went in.

Richelle, Liz, and Sunny were sitting on the bed, just shadows in the dark.

"Can't you sleep, either?" Liz asked us.

"What do you think?" Nick grunted. "Who could sleep in this creepy house?"

"No offense, Elmo," said Sunny. "But he's right."

"Listen," I said. "I agree with you. But I don't think it's Aunt Vivien's fault."

So then we all started talking. And the more we talked, the more fishy the whole thing seemed.

On the one hand, we were told Aunt Vivien had forgotten we were coming. On the other hand, the beds were all made, and the pantry was stacked with food.

On the one hand, Aunt Vivien did appear to be sick. On the other hand, she'd been wanting to meet me. She'd said so in her letters. So you'd think that she'd be trying to talk to me, however sick she felt.

"It's really strange," whispered Liz. "It's as if —"

Then, suddenly, there was a crash and a bloodcurdling yell. We all leaped up as if we'd been shot.

"What was that?" whimpered Richelle.

"Someone's fallen over or something," suggested Liz.

We rushed out of the bedroom and felt our way down the stairs from the mezzanine, to the room with the big round table.

Now we could hear movement, and long, low groans. Somewhere in the house, someone was in pain.

Nick stopped, and listened. "It's coming from in there," he said, pointing at the heavy carved door that led to the tower wing.

"It must be Aunt Vivien," I exclaimed.

I skirted the table and fumbled my way to the door. I felt for the handle, turned it, shook it. It was locked.

Suddenly, I had a terrible feeling. I banged on the door. "Aunt Vivien!" I yelled. "Are you all right?"

"Elmo!" warned Liz. "Not so loud."

Outside there was a flash of lightning, and a huge clap of thunder.

And at that same moment, the heavy door clicked, as a key was turned in its lock. It swung open with a hideous creak.

Mrs. Never-dead was standing there, with a flashlight in her hand.

I heard Richelle give a squeal of fright. The woman was frowning with anger. She shone the flashlight in my face.

"What are you doing out of bed?" she asked sternly.

I don't know why we should have been scared of her. After all, we were in my aunt's house. And Mrs. Never-dead was only the housekeeper. But we *were* scared of her.

"We . . . heard someone screaming," I quavered, blinking in the light.

"Well, it's no concern of yours. Miss Zimmer had a bad nightmare. But she's all right now. There's nothing to worry about. Go back to bed."

What else could we do? She stood watching us as we trailed back up the stairs to the mezzanine. Then she slammed the door, and we heard the lock click again as the key was turned.

"I think we should go back to bed, like she says," whispered Nick. "Everything seems quiet now."

"I want to see if Aunt Vivien's all right!" I said fiercely.

Liz patted my arm. "It probably was just a nightmare, Elmo," she said.

"And think about it," Sunny added. "We don't know this house, and we haven't got a flashlight. You'll just have to wait till morning, and talk to Aunt Vivien then."

What she said was sensible. I could see that.

We said good night for the second time and went back to our rooms. I changed again, and crawled back into bed. But as I lay in bed, listening to the thunderstorm raging outside, I wasn't happy.

I didn't believe the nightmare story. Not for a minute. Now I knew for sure there was something really wrong. Aunt Vivien was in trouble.

I lay awake for hours, tossing and turning. The thunderstorm had long passed, and it was starting to get light by the time I fell asleep.

I'd expected to be woken early. After all, this was the country, and we were going to be working. But it was past nine o'clock when I opened my eyes. Sunlight was flooding through the thin slit of my window.

I lay there, blinking. Just for a moment, I didn't quite know where I was.

Then I remembered. The screams in the night. The storm. Mrs. Never-dead shining the flashlight in my face and ordering us back to bed.

Everything seemed terribly quiet. I got out of bed and quickly pulled on my clothes. My heart had started hammering. Where was everyone? What had happened?

But nothing had happened. Everyone had just slept in. Nick came out of his room at the same time I came out of mine, looking tired and crabby. Behind his own door, Tom was thumping around, complaining to himself as he got dressed. We waited for him, and then went down to the mezzanine, to see what the others were doing.

They were in Liz's room, talking. Just exactly as they'd been last night. Except that now it was light, and I could see the dark circles under their eyes. They'd obviously slept as poorly as we had.

"Breakfast," said Tom firmly, and they nodded.

We shuffled downstairs, hardly speaking. I glanced at the heavy carved door as we reached the room with the big round table. I wondered what had been going on behind it last night. I wondered what was going to happen today.

8

Horrors

The Never-deads, looking rather the worse for wear after their busy night, were drinking coffee at the kitchen table when we came in. When they saw us, they both stood up. Mr. Never-dead turned his back and looked out the window.

"Good morning," the woman said. "You'll find a box of cereal in the pantry, and milk in the left-hand refrigerator."

So breakfast was going to be cereal and milk. After last night, none of us had really expected a big country breakfast. But when I opened the fridge to get out the milk and saw all the goodies inside, I could have cried.

There was a leg of ham. There were eggs and bacon. There was a huge bowl of fruit salad. There were melons and grapes and bottles of orange juice. There was cream.

The pantry was stacked to the rafters with cans and packages. I turned my face away from them and sadly pulled out the giant-size box of cereal from the bottom shelf.

I carried it to the table. Sunny had already gotten bowls and spoons for everyone. Everyone else sat down and helped themselves eagerly. But I looked at Mrs. Never-dead, who was standing by the sink.

"How's Aunt Vivien?" I asked her.

"Not too bad, considering," the woman said.

"I'd like to see her, please," I said, as politely as I could. "If she's not well, I could go to her room."

Mrs. Never-dead hesitated for a moment. Then with a sigh she clattered her cup into the sink.

"That won't be necessary," she snapped. "She'll be down shortly. Just have your breakfast."

She strode out of the kitchen. Her husband stayed where he was, hands in pockets, staring out at the view.

We had two huge bowls of cereal each. We were all starving.

In a way, I wouldn't have been surprised if Mrs. Never-dead had come back saying that Aunt Vivien had gone back to sleep. For some reason she obviously wasn't eager to let me see her. But I guess she'd decided I wasn't going to quit so easily, because we'd just finished our second bowl of cereal when Aunt Vivien came in.

She looked much the same as she had yesterday, except that she was wearing sunglasses.

"The morning sun hurts your aunt's eyes," said Mrs. Never-dead, frowning at my curious look. "Isn't that right, Miss Zimmer?"

"Yes," murmured Aunt Vivien, and sniffed. Mrs. Never-dead guided her toward a chair at one end of the table, and she sank down into it as if she was exhausted.

"Good morning, Aunt Vivien," I said, as cheerily as I could.

She smiled at me and fiddled uncertainly with a loose button on her cardigan.

"Are you going to have some breakfast, Miss Zimmer?" asked Tom, seeing an opportunity for more food, and seizing it. "There's some nice-looking ham in the fridge."

Aunt Vivien turned her head to look at him. And as she did, I saw behind the side of her glasses.

I shivered in horror. The old woman had a black eye!

"I heard you call out last night," I said loudly. "I was worried about you."

Aunt Vivien opened her mouth to speak, but Mrs. Never-dead cut in with a forced laugh before she could say a word. "It was just a nightmare, wasn't it, Miss Zimmer?"

Aunt Vivien's shoulders slumped, and she nodded silently.

I saw the Never-deads exchanging meaningful looks.

"Well," said the man, "time for you kids to get to work. Weeding the front yard. Right?"

Aunt Vivien was staring down at the tabletop.

"Aunt Vivien . . ." I began. But she didn't offer any sign that she'd heard me.

Sunny tugged at my arm. "Let's go, Elmo," she muttered.

I met her eyes. They were serious and watchful. And they were sending me a message.

I saw what you saw, those eyes were saying. *Let's get out where we can talk.*

We went out to the front yard and started pulling out weeds. Mr. Never-dead watched us for a while, then wandered off.

As soon as we were alone, Sunny and I told the others about Aunt Vivien's black eye.

"Maybe she got it falling out of bed," Tom suggested.

I shook my head. "I don't think so. It didn't look just like an ordinary cut or a bruise."

Sunny nodded her agreement.

"But they couldn't really have been *harming* her, could they?" breathed Richelle. "I mean, she's just an old lady."

"It happens," I said grimly. "She might have bruises on her arms and legs as well, hidden under her clothes."

"But why?" frowned Nick. "Why would they be hurting her?"

I shivered. "I don't know. All I know is, she's scared to death of them. You can see it. That woman talks for her. Won't let her be alone with us. And Aunt Vivien doesn't even try. Those two have got her completely beaten."

"This is *terrible*," Liz hissed. "What are we going to do?"

"Whatever it is, we'll have to be careful," said Sunny. "We don't want to make things worse for her."

"Maybe we should wait till we get home, and then tell Zim," Richelle put in.

"We won't be getting home till Monday afternoon, Richelle!" Liz exploded. "We can't leave her in this situation till then."

"We've got to get her alone," I said. "Talk to her. Find out what's going on. Tell her we'll help her."

"Yeah," Tom agreed. "But that means getting rid of the Never-deads. And that's not going to be easy."

We spread out and started pulling weeds again. We worked for five minutes without stopping. But all the time we were moving farther and farther away from the kitchen side of the house. Eventually, we knew, we'd be out of sight. Then we could talk properly.

I looked up after a while and saw that Nick was beckoning to me. With a quick glance at the kitchen door — all clear — I ran over to him.

Nick was holding a piece of paper. It had been crumpled up, but he'd flattened it out again. He held it out to me.

It was a poster about Saturday night's wrestling match. Exactly like the one Tom had decorated at the Kneebone station. Except that this one was stained, and it had none of Tom's improvements.

I frowned at Nick as the others gathered around to see what he was showing me.

"So?" I asked him.

"So look at that," he said impatiently, and flicked the paper with his finger. "What does it say?"

I read the words under the pictures of the Roman gladiator and the monster man sizing up one another.

THE KILLER vs. THE FREAK

TWO DEADLY ENEMIES LOCKED IN FIGHT TO THE DEATH.

KNEEBONE TOWN HALL, SATURDAY NIGHT.
BE THERE!

"What's the big deal?" asked Tom, looking over my shoulder. "A poster smeared with tomato sauce."

"I found it just now, on the grass by the wall of the house," Nick said.

"Maybe Mr. Never-dead planned to go to the match," Tom said. "But now that he's getting his kicks from beating up old ladies, he's lost interest. We should get him for littering."

"Yes," said Richelle. "The pig! And he dropped it this morning, too. I cleaned up around the tower yesterday. No way I would have missed it."

"Look, you dopes, Never-dead didn't drop this! Can't you see?" Nick stabbed at the paper impatiently.

I looked at the grubby paper again, and suddenly I saw what he meant. The tomato sauce marks formed a pattern. They'd been carefully smeared on the paper, probably by someone's finger.

Some of the words had been highlighted. They leaped out at me, glowing red. And they were followed by a ragged "V."

I noticed something else, too. Something that made my stomach turn over.

"It's a message," breathed Liz. "And that drip-mark there at the end of the middle line. It's a 'V,' isn't it?"

"Yes," I said grimly. "'V' for Vivien."

Liz looked closely at the paper and sniffed.

When she looked up again, she had a curious expression on her face.

"You know, this doesn't smell like tomato sauce," she said slowly.

I shook my head. I felt sick.

"That's because it's not tomato sauce," I said grimly.

9

The plan

"She's sent us a coded message," I continued. I was proud of Aunt Vivien just then. I'd said the Never-deads had her beaten. But they didn't.

They were stopping her from asking us for help directly. But she'd found a way of doing it secretly. It must have taken a lot of courage. She was a real Zimmer all right, whatever Grandad had thought.

"See?" I pointed to the words that had been smeared with blood. "It's the middle line that's been marked."

Liz read the glowing, highlighted words and the signature that followed.

TWO DEADLY ENEMIES ...
FIGHT TO THE DEATH. V.

There was a short, breathless silence as we took this in.

"Well, we know one thing now," Sunny said, after a moment. "These people aren't just playing around."

"How did she get hold of the poster, do you think?" asked Richelle.

"I reckon it must have fallen out of old Never-dead's pocket," Tom said.

"So she found it, and got away somewhere on her own. Then she marked the poster and tossed it out of one of the upstairs windows, hoping we'd find it," Liz said. "A bathroom window, maybe. They'd let her go to the bathroom alone, surely."

We all looked up. And high above us there was a small window, right near the top of the tower.

"I can't believe this is really happening," moaned Richelle.

I crumpled up the note and stuffed it into my pocket. I was shaking all over. It was shock, I suppose. And anger. And pity for this poor, terrified old lady I hardly knew, but who'd been my own grandad's little sister.

"We've got to do something," I said, through gritted teeth. "And we have to let her know we've gotten her message."

"We will, Elmo," Liz said, putting an arm around my shoulders. "But we must not panic. We have to plan."

We moved a bit farther away from the house. We kept pulling weeds, so we'd look as though we were still working. But we stood close enough to each other to talk.

"Okay. Now. We can't all just disappear and rush off to get help at Kneebone," Sunny said. "The Never-deads might suspect something. They might . . . hurt her again."

I winced. But I knew she was right.

"We have to pretend we don't know anything," I agreed.

"So we split up," Liz put in. "We send one person into town to get help, and cover for him, or her. Pretend that person's still here. Sunny's the best runner, so she should be it."

"She shouldn't go alone," Nick objected.

"She'll have to," I said. "It'll be hard enough covering for one person. We'd never cover for two or more."

"I'll be fine," said Sunny calmly. "But how are you going to make sure they don't realize I've gone?"

"You can pretend to be sick, or faint or something," suggested Liz. "We could pretend to take you up to your bedroom to sleep. . . ."

"So they think I'm in my room while I climb out of a window and take off for town," Sunny chimed in.

"I still think someone should go with you," Nick insisted.

"We've been through that!" I snapped, impatient at the delay. "The rest of us have things to do here. We have to fool the Never-deads, and we have to protect Aunt Vivien."

"It's not going to be easy," said Liz doubtfully.

"Well, if this group can't do it, no one can," I said. "Nick and Richelle are good at being nice and well-mannered to people when they don't mean it —"

"Thanks a lot," drawled Nick. But Richelle smiled. She took it as a compliment.

"Tom's good at acting —" I went on.

"Lying, you mean," Nick interrupted.

"I learn all the best things from you," Tom said.

"And," I said, raising my voice, "Liz is the perfect person to make Aunt Vivien feel better. She's good with old people. And she's good at comforting."

Liz looked at me sideways. She wasn't sure if she wanted to be seen as Little Miss Comforter.

"What about you?" she demanded.

"Oh, General Elmo will direct operations from his bed," Nick said.

"While eating ice cream," Tom added.

"And wearing silk PJs," Richelle said.

"I'll find something to do," I said, and managed to laugh, though I didn't feel much like it. I knew they were trying to make me feel better.

"So. When do we do this?" asked Sunny.

"Soon," I said. "But I think we ought to work up to it."

"That's right," Liz agreed enthusiastically. "We really want the Never-deads to believe you're sick, Sunny. So let's go inside and get them into the mood."

"I'm not much good at acting," said Sunny doubtfully.

"It's easy," exclaimed Richelle. "All you have to do is think about being sick. Tell yourself you feel faint and woozy and that you look pale and everything. And before you know it, you will! I do it all the time. When I want to."

"Me, too," agreed Tom.

Sunny glanced at them in disbelief.

Liz sighed. "Just keep quiet, and try to pretend you're very, very tired, Sunny," she said. "We'll do the rest."

We went cautiously into the kitchen. The Never-deads weren't there.

But luck was on our side. We got to the kitchen just in time to overhear a very interesting conversation.

The Never-deads were in the next room, and couldn't see us. They were talking. And we could hear every word.

"Now, don't lose your nerve, Kevin," Mrs. Never-dead was saying. "Once we get those kids out of here, there'll be nothing to worry about."

"I s'pose so," he said. "But the old lady's a toughie."

"Toughie, nothing," Mrs. Never-dead said. "She's an old woman. She'll crack in the end."

"Maybe," Mr. Never-dead said. "But we don't want those bratty kids getting antsy and telling their parents."

"Right," she agreed. "And speaking of antsy, it's about time Aunt Vivien made another appearance. Otherwise, they *will* start to wonder. We'll call them in for some morning tea, and I'll bring her down."

"It's a bit risky," Mr. Never-dead grumbled.

"Don't *worry*, Kevin," snapped the woman. "I'll be with them every second."

"What if they see that black eye?"

"They won't. Everything'll be okay as long as we don't leave them alone," Mrs. Never-dead said. "It'll take only five minutes — enough to satisfy them. Then we'll send them off to do another job. We'll work them hard all day. Give them so much to do they can't think about anything."

We heard their footsteps walking away. And slowly their voices faded. They'd gone to another part of the house.

"What *can* they be after?" Liz asked, looking at me.

"I've got no idea," I said. "But Aunt Vivien has got money. At least, Grandad always said she had. Maybe it's that."

"Maybe the Never-deads want her to change her will in their favor," Tom said.

"Or maybe there's something valuable hidden in the house," Richelle suggested. "You know. Fabulous jewelry. They could be trying to make her tell them where it is."

"Or there could be something on the land. Or under it," Nick said. "Oil. Gold. A diamond mine. Something like that. And they're wanting her to sell the land to them."

"It doesn't really matter what they want, does it?" I broke in. "What matters is that they're dangerous."

"Aunt Vivien should have been more careful who she hired," said Tom.

"I don't think she did," I said flatly. "I don't think they're really Aunt Vivien's housekeeper and farm manager."

"I've been thinking the same thing," said Nick. "For a start, they couldn't have been here very long, or they'd have known about the trains."

"Yes," said Liz. "And if the Never-deads were real house-help, Aunt Vivien wouldn't need us to get the yard and stuff all tidied up. Would she?"

"And what about the letters?" Tom added. "They obviously hadn't seen those. Or they'd have known we were coming. So they must have come here since Aunt Vivien got Zim's last letter. Only a couple of days ago."

"And she wouldn't have told them about us," I put in. "We were her last chance of being rescued. Looks like we got here just in time."

The kitchen door swung open. Mr. Never-dead stood there, scowling at us.

"Just in time?" he said angrily. "What do you mean by that?"

10

Finders keepers

The man strode into the kitchen. My throat went dry. How much had he heard?

"What d'you mean, 'just in time'?" he repeated.

"I —" I hesitated. I didn't know what to say.

"Yeah. We came in just in time to stop ourselves from dying of thirst," grinned Tom, ambling over to the sink as if he didn't have a worry in the world.

I couldn't help admiring him. Call it acting, or call it lying, he was very good at it.

"Oh, right," growled Mr. Never-dead.

He looked behind him, then stood aside to let his wife lead Aunt Vivien into the room.

"Sit down, Miss Zimmer," said the woman with that terrible, fake smile. She pushed Aunt Vivien down onto one of the kitchen chairs. "Now. Would you like a nice cup of tea?"

Aunt Vivien nodded. "Yes, please," she said in a low voice.

"The children have been working very hard," chattered Mrs. Never-dead, filling the kettle at the sink. "They've been doing some weeding this morning."

"Oh, that's nice," whispered the old woman. She sniffed and dabbed her nose with what looked like the same crumpled tissue she'd been using yesterday.

She looked so sad and uncomfortable. She kept looking at me, nervously, pretending to smile.

I smiled back. Then I thought of a way to let her know we'd picked up her message.

"We were thinking," I said, in a chatty sort of way. "We might all go to the amateur wrestling match at Kneebone tonight. Wouldn't that be fun?"

"Wrestling?" Richelle sneered. "Dirty, ugly, sweaty wrestlers half-killing each other? Fun?"

"Yeah, fun," Tom growled, giving Richelle a little kick in the ankle.

"Maybe Aunt Vivien would like to come, too," I said. "If she's feeling better."

For the first time, Aunt Vivien's eyes brightened and she smiled properly. It was just a little smile. But I knew she'd gotten the message.

"Of course Miss Zimmer wouldn't want to go," Mrs. Never-dead snorted. "And she couldn't walk all that way, even if she did."

"I don't think we should go, either," said Liz casually. "Sunny's not feeling too well. Are you, Sunny?"

Sunny self-consciously shook her head.

Mrs. Never-dead frowned. "What's the matter with you?" she asked Sunny sharply.

Sunny looked down at her hands.

"She might be getting the flu," said Tom. "There's a lot of it going around."

Mrs. Never-dead's frown deepened. "I hope not," she scowled. "That would be *very* inconvenient."

"I think they ought to get on with the work now," Mr. Never-dead urged, looking at her. He was getting edgy. He wanted us out of the kitchen. Away from Aunt Vivien.

His wife clicked her tongue impatiently, but nodded. "Yes," she said. "Miss Zimmer needs a bit of peace to drink her tea. You people pop back outside and clean out the Rolls garage. Off you go now."

Mr. Never-dead opened the back door, and we filed through. I managed to give Aunt Vivien another smile as I passed her.

At least, I thought, *she knows now that we're on to them. And that we'll do something to help.*

As soon as we were outside, Mr. Never-dead hustled us around to the back of the house and pointed at the garage. "Okay," he growled. "You'd better get started. And no messing around. There's lots more work for you to do before the day's over."

He was right there. But it wasn't the sort of work he had in mind.

The back of the garage was piled high with junk. Bits of old beds. Rusty paint tins. Piles of old newspapers and magazines. You name it, Aunt Vivien had stuck it in the garage. There were also the shelves of papers that climbed up the side walls to the roof.

"Clear out the whole garage," said Mr. Never-dead. "We'll sort through it later."

He pointed to a clear space in the yard. "You can pile it up out there. And you can clean the Rolls while you're at it."

perfect working order. Or there's the SUV, if you'd prefer. Big green thing. They've probably put it in the garage next to the Rolls."

"A shiny green SUV?" I asked slowly.

She nodded.

"A green SUV passed us on the way here," said Sunny.

"That's right," said Richelle. "The driver was drinking a can of Coke. I could have killed him for it."

"The driver was a man with a ponytail," I said.

I suddenly saw it all. The light had finally dawned.

It was him. The man with the ponytail was the fake Aunt Vivien. He'd been Mrs. Never-dead's solution to the problem of Help-for-Hire turning up at just the wrong moment.

The long hair was real. So the fake Aunt Vivien had fooled us completely. Richelle would have spotted a wig in a second.

"How," said Aunt Vivien severely, "you could ever have thought that ridiculous man was me, I can't imagine."

I bit my lip. "I didn't know what you looked like," I mumbled.

"He brought me some food last night. Still dressed in that horrible get-up she'd made him put on," Aunt Vivien fumed. "I was so mad that as soon as he untied my hands so I could eat, I punched him in the eye."

There was a shout of laughter from the gang.

"We . . . we heard a scream in the night. We saw the black eye the next day. We thought the Never-deads were roughing you up," I stammered. "And all the time it was you doing the damage. I don't believe it!"

"Anyway," said Aunt Vivien. "Take the car —"

"But . . . um . . . none of us can drive," I cut in.

"Do I have to do *everything* myself?" she asked briskly. "I have to stay here. I don't trust those nasty customers upstairs."

While we were thinking about that, we heard a siren. Coming closer.

"Must be a fire somewhere," said Aunt Vivien.

Then I remembered. "Yes!" I yelled. "It worked! Hey, it worked!"

"What worked?" everyone asked.

"Come and see!"

Outside, in the backyard, the pile of junk we'd moved from the garage was burning like mad. It was a huge blaze. The fire I'd lit, in the few seconds I had between running away from the Never-deads and giving myself up again, had really taken hold.

Up the Mistfall driveway roared two fire engines and a police car, sirens blaring.

Elmo's fire. Not as romantic as Saint Elmo's fire, maybe. But more successful as protection.

Just as I'd hoped, the bonfire had drawn more attention to Mistfall than a hundred people going for help.

The police and fire brigade — and I guess everyone for miles around — had been able to see the blaze. It was huge.

"Elmo," said Aunt Vivien, squeezing my shoulder, "you're a smart thinker. You're a real Zimmer, after all."

While the firefighters put out the bonfire, the police came in to see if everything was okay. It turned out they were friends of Aunt Vivien.

"Well, well, well," said the sergeant, when we showed them the three tied-up crooks. "I do believe it's old 'Sniffer' Brindley behind that black eye."

"You know him, George?" asked Aunt Vivien.

"Know him?" he echoed. "He'd qualify for the *Guinness Book of Records* as the stupidest small-time crook this side of the Mississippi. And who are these two? Let's have a look at them."

Mr. and Mrs. Never-dead stood silently with their heads down. Aunt Vivien took one head in each hand and jerked them up for the sergeant to see.

"Ha! I might have known," he said. "The Everedds. Brother and sister. Got a record as long as my arm, and wanted in a couple of states, to boot."

He told the two officers with him to take the Everedds away.

"Viv," he said to my great-aunt, after they'd gone, "get a phone line installed, will you? You can't go lighting fires every time you want to call the cops."

Heavy footsteps pounded the floorboards in the hall. I guess I was still very nervous. *Lucky the police are still in the house*, I thought.

It was the two big guys from the train. A little guy was with them.

"We were on our way to Kneebone when we saw the fire," one of the big guys said.

"Yeah," said the other. "Thought you might need some help. What happened?"

The sergeant explained and thanked them for stopping.

"Hey," said one of the big guys. "Aren't you the kids who came up on the same train as us?"

We nodded.

"Well, don't let a little thing like this spoil your weekend."

He turned to the little guy. "Got any tickets?"

The little guy put his hand in the inside pocket of his coat.

"Got a few spare ones, Bill," he said.

"How'd ya like to come to the wrestling match?" said Bill.

"I'd *love* to," said Aunt Vivien, before any of the rest of us had a chance to say anything.

"You're on!" grinned Bill. "Jumbo and I are on tonight at Kneebone town hall. Y'know? The Killer and The Freak?"

I couldn't believe it. These guys were deadly *enemies*? They seemed like the best of friends.

"Aren't you supposed to fight to the death?" asked Richelle, staring at them.

The wrestlers laughed.

"That's right," Bill said. "We always fight to the death, don't we, Jumbo?"

"Yeah. That's right," said Jumbo. "Sometimes he dies. Sometimes I die. Ask our manager."

They roared with laughter and slapped each other on the back. Bill, their manager, just nodded and laughed with them.

"See you later," Frank said.

"Yeah," Bill said. "It's his turn to die tonight."

They were still laughing as they got into the big black car and drove away.

17

Answers

We sat around the kitchen table after everyone had gone. Aunt Vivien raided the fridge and pantry and plunked everything down. Ham, tomatoes, potato salad, chicken, ice cream, cakes, drinks, potato chips — everything she could lay her hands on.

It was a feast. And for a while, we did nothing but eat.

Then Aunt Vivien reached over and patted Sunny's hand.

"You've got a useful friend here," she said. "She's very quick on her feet. Sniffer nabbed her, trying to slip out."

Sunny made a face. She wasn't very proud of being caught. "The Never-deads were in the kitchen. I thought they were the only ones I had to watch out for," she said. "I was just getting through a back window, when he grabbed me."

Aunt Vivien took up the story. "Anyway, he tied her up and dumped her in the tower room, with me. Then he ran off to tell the Everedds."

She smiled with remembered pleasure, and took a spoonful of chocolate ice cream.

"By the time he came back to check on us, after the lights went out, we were ready for him. We'd untied each other. We tackled him as he came through the door. Knocked him out. Then we tied him up and left him there. Oh, Sunny was a brave little soldier."

Sunny isn't good at being praised. She didn't say anything.

"We holed up. We were going to wait for our chance to pick off the Never-deads, as you call them, one by one," Aunt Vivien went on. "We couldn't take any risks. I knew they had weapons. That's how they caught me in the first place."

Sunny grinned. "But then everything got complicated," she said. "People running around. Odd noises. Then they had you as hostages. We had to be very careful. So we stayed hidden till the time was right. Vivien worked it all out."

I could see by the look on her face that she thought my Aunt Vivien was a pretty brave soldier, too.

But we all wanted to know more. In fact, I for one had about a thousand questions to ask. I settled for the most important one.

"Why did the Everedds come here?" I asked.

Aunt Vivien held her head up. Her lined face was proud, and her eyes were bright and sharp. I'd seen the same expression on Grandad's face.

Like she said — how could I have thought for a second that Sniffer Brindley was the real Vivien Zimmer?

"Elmo, you heard about me from your grandfather, didn't you?" she asked.

I nodded and felt myself blushing. She smiled.

"You've heard how silly and selfish I am, and how I've traveled around the world all my life, just living it up?" she persisted.

"Um — sort of," I mumbled.

"Well," said Aunt Vivien cheerfully, "that's what everyone

thought. I'm retired now. So there's no harm telling you, though I'd ask you to keep it under your hats. Up until a few years ago, I was what you might call a secret agent."

"Wow," said Tom. "You mean a spy?"

She grinned at him. "In a way. Mostly it was pretty ordinary stuff. Passing messages. Delivering packages. Microfilm. That sort of stuff."

"Weren't you worried about getting caught?" asked Richelle. "Spies often get caught in the movies."

"They often did, and still do, in real life," Aunt Vivien said. "It's a risk one has to take. But if you worry about getting caught, you might as well give it up."

She grinned again. "But I was lucky. No one suspected me. Not even my brother, Elmo's grandfather. He was always terribly snobby about my traveling. Thought I should have settled down and raised a family, like he did. But that wasn't my style. And, of course, I couldn't tell him what I was really doing."

I could hardly believe what I was hearing. But I knew I had to. "So, if you've retired now, why did the Everedds take you prisoner, Aunt Vivien?" I asked.

She shrugged. "Because they're incredibly stupid people," she said.

We stared at her. Tom helped himself to more ham, and a chicken leg to go with it.

"Stories make me hungry," he explained, when Liz frowned at him.

"It was like this," said Aunt Vivien. "A few months ago, a very dear friend from the old days was in this country, and he came to see me. Sniffer Brindley — one of the local bad apples, as you must have gathered — overheard a conversation I had with this friend. We were in the Kneebone Diner, remembering the old days.

"We talked about a huge stash of gold bars we'd once been involved with. Many, many years ago, after World War II."

She smiled, her eyes full of memories. "I won't tell you the details," she went on. "Enough to say that the gold was in a safe in a Swiss bank. My friend had one key. I had the other. The safe could only be opened by using both keys together. My friend had brought his key with him. And that night in the hotel he gave it to me, as a keepsake."

Liz's eyes were dreamy with romance. But I could see that Nick was on the edge of his chair. I knew what he wanted to know. I wanted to know it, too.

"And do you still have your key, Aunt Vivien?" I asked.

"That's what the Everedds were after," she said. "Sniffer Brindley was somehow connected with them, and he told them what he'd heard and seen in the hotel. So they came here and held me prisoner. They wanted to go and get the gold, you see."

She grinned, and for a moment, she looked very young. "I had my friend's key. But the truth is, I don't know where my own key is. I really don't. I know I put it away somewhere safe, but I've completely forgotten where. I couldn't have told the Everedds where it was to save my life."

I dug into my jeans pocket and pulled out the key that had been tied to the little box Richelle found in the Rolls.

"Is this it?" I asked, and told her where we'd found it.

She stared at it. "You know, I think it is," she said slowly, turning it over in her hand.

"That means you can go to Switzerland and get the gold," Nick said. I'd swear that he was already deciding how to spend his share.

Aunt Vivien laughed a very hearty laugh.

"Oh, if only," she said. "But after the war, the Swiss bank released it to the proper government of the country concerned, without worrying about the keys. There hasn't been any gold in that safe for ages!"

"Why didn't you tell the Everedds that?" Liz asked.

"I did, Liz. Over and over. Till I was sick of the sound of my own voice. But they thought I was lying."

"They *were* pretty stupid, then, weren't they?" said Nick. He was handling his disappointment well, I thought.

"Stupid!" Aunt Vivien exclaimed. "Stupid isn't the word for it. But anyway, they're out of the way now. And I suggest we change our clothes, and go watch some wrestling now."

"In the *Rolls?*" exclaimed Richelle, clasping her hands with delight.

"Certainly," said Aunt Vivien, licking the last of the chocolate ice cream from her lips. "How else?"

On Sunday, we had a huge lunch. The wrestlers, the police sergeant, and some other friends of Aunt Vivien's joined us. It was a great party. And we loved every minute of it.

When it was time to leave for the train on Monday, Aunt Vivien paid us three times what we would have been paid if we'd worked the entire time we were there.

We looked at each other. Liz spoke for us all.

"We can't take it," she said. "We haven't worked for it. Well, not for as much as that."

"Don't be ridiculous," cried Aunt Vivien. "Haven't you heard of hazard pay? I insist that you take it."

So we did. As Nick said, who's going to argue with a woman like Aunt Vivien?

At the station, Aunt Vivien gave everyone in the gang a big hug and thanked them.

Then she hugged me. "It's good to know you at last, Elmo," she said. "In your own way, you're as handy as Sunny. You're a real thinker. Lighting that fire was a stroke of genius. Come and see me again. Will you?"

"Of course I will," I said.

She gave me another hug.

"Give my regards to your father. You can tell him about me if you like. Then he might understand why I've kept away from the family all these years."

Just as the train was starting, I put my head out the window and asked her one last question.

"If you'd known where the other key was, and if the gold was still in the vault, would you have told the Never-deads?"

She looked at me scornfully.

"Of course not, you silly boy. Would you?"

I didn't answer. The train pulled away from the station.

"No, of course you wouldn't," she called after it, waving. "You're a real Zimmer, Saint Elmo."

And that thought kept me happy all the long way home.

Want to know what happens next?
Here's a sneak peek from:

EMILY RODDA'S
RAVEN HILL MYSTERIES

CASE #5: DIRTY TRICKS

EMILY RODDA'S
RAVEN HILL MYSTERIES

CASE #5: DIRTY TRICKS

It all started at Raven Hill High — in class, one cold, rainy, wintry Monday morning. Our new student English teacher, Mr. Raven, was giving us an assignment. As if a rainy Monday morning wasn't back luck enough.

Mr. Raven was weird. He wore a dark suit and black-framed rectangular glasses. He was very thin and pale, and he had straight, shoulder-length black hair and big, pale green eyes.

He didn't look like your average student teacher, in other words. He didn't seem to have that awful, bright enthusiasm that most student teachers have, either. His voice was soft and low and never changed tone at all. It never went up, and it never went down.

In fact, there was something quite spooky about him. A few of the guys at the back of the class had tried to give him a hard time early in the lesson. But he'd just kind of looked at them with those pale green eyes and they shut up.

He handed out photocopied sheets to everyone. I looked at my copy. It was headed "Alphabetical Mysteries." Underneath was a list of words in alphabetical order: *Alphabet, Bees, Chameleon, Doughnut,* and so on, all the way down to *Zodiac.*

Mr. Raven told us that, as there were twenty-six of us in the class, and twenty-six letters in the alphabet, there was one topic on the list for each of us.

"A most fortunate coincidence," he said softly, pushing his hair behind his ears with long, bony fingers. "I am very fond of the alphabet." His thin lips curved in what I guess was a smile. It was a weird, curvy smile that didn't show his teeth.

I looked at Liz and Nick, who were sitting on my left. We've been stuck with some weird teachers before, but it looked like Mr. Raven was going to be the worst yet. Nick rolled his eyes back at me, and Liz covered a smile with her hand.

"You are each to choose one of these topics, and research it at Raven Hill Library," Mr. Raven went on. "It's very important to develop good library skills. It is also good to support your local library by using it regularly."

"And by paying library fines," groaned Tom on my right, as he sketched cartoons of Mr. Raven all over his list of topics. I pretended I hadn't heard him. For days we'd been hearing about Tom's lost library book, and getting updates of everywhere he'd looked for it. I never listened when he got started. If only he'd be a bit more organized he wouldn't get himself into these messes.

"As I told you all when I introduced myself," continued Mr. Raven, perching carefully on the edge of his desk, "until a few weeks ago I worked part-time at Raven Hill Library. So I know that they have books on all these topics."

I gazed at the clock helplessly and listened to the rain beating down outside. I hate assignments. And these topics were really weird. E for Elephant. F for Fingerprint. G for Gypsy. Apart from the fact that they were all in a list together, they seemed to have nothing in common.

Fortunately, I wasn't the only one who was confused.

"These topics are all very different from one another, Mr. Raven," said Sunny's flat, practical voice from the row in front of me. "I don't really understand what we have to do."

Mr. Raven gave that strange little smile again and sat up straighter on the edge of his desk.

"The assignment title is the clue," he said. "'Alphabetical Mysteries.' You'll find that every one of the topics on this list involves some kind of mystery."

A flash of lightning lit up the room and I jumped. He paused until the thunder crashed a second or two later, and a shiver ran up and down my spine. He didn't have to be so dark and spooky in the middle of a storm! Not when there were people as sensitive as me in the class. I get spooked really easily.

"Mystery?" said Elmo, who was sitting next to Sunny. I could see him leaning forward on his desk. I could just imagine his eyes sparkling. Trust Elmo to be interested.

Mr. Raven nodded. "There is something about each of these topics that is not widely known, or not fully understood, or is just surprising or unusual," he said.

"So how come P is for Phobia instead of Phantom?" some idiot called out from the back. Bradley Henshaw, probably.

Everyone snickered. Thanks to our local paper, the *Pen*, everyone knew about the so-called Phantom of the Library, and the tricks he had been playing for the last month. Everyone thought they were so funny. Everyone but me, that is.

Mr. Raven ignored the interruption. "I have my own ideas," he went on. "But it's up to each of you to choose your topic and then discover and describe the mystery that *you* see within it."

It sounded pretty boring to me. I looked at the list again. I couldn't see anything mysterious about most of these topics. Elephants? Elephants are elephants. Doughnut? What's mysterious about a doughnut? It's fattening. It's round. That's all.

"When's it due?" asked Nick, getting down to basics.

"Next Monday," answered Mr. Raven briefly.

Just a week! There was a bit of complaining about that, but he raised his hand for silence. "The research won't take long," he said calmly. "Then you need only write as much as you need to explain the mystery. And give a list of the books you've used to discover it."

I wriggled uncomfortably on my chair.

"I suggest you waste no time in choosing your topic," said Mr. Raven as the bell rang. I sprang to my feet in relief. I couldn't wait to get out of there.

To my surprise, most of the other kids crowded around Mr. Raven's desk, trying to get in first with their choices. Some of them seemed really excited.

"X! X! I want X!" I heard Tom yell. I checked my sheet. X-ray.

"X-ray. Of course. It couldn't be anything else. Except Xylophone, I suppose," I said gloomily.

"What about Xylem? Or Xenophobia?" asked Elmo.

I nodded to make it seem like I knew what those words

meant, and left without putting my name down for anything. The thunder rumbled loudly, like a warning that trouble lay ahead.

I should have listened to it.

To be continued . . .

Thrilling tales of adventure and danger...

Emily Rodda's

∾ DELTORA ∾

Enter the realm of monsters, mayhem, and magic of Deltora Quest, Deltora Shadowlands, and Dragons of Deltora

Gordon Korman's

ON THE RUN

The chase is on in this heart-stopping series about two fugitive kids who must follow a trail of clues to prove their parents' innocence.

Gregor the Overlander
by Suzanne Collins

In the Underland, Gregor must face giant talking cockroaches, rideable bats, and a legendary Rat King to save his family, himself, and maybe the entire subterranean world.

Available wherever you buy books.

■ SCHOLASTIC

FILLBOY6

WHO'S BEHIND THE PRANKS IN THE LIBRARY?

EMILY RODDA'S
RAVEN HILL MYSTERIES

#5: DIRTY TRICKS

■SCHOLASTIC

The Help-for-Hire gang has too much homework! The local library seems like a great place to hit the books—until the books start hitting back. The Phantom of the Library is playing practical jokes. But as the tricks turn more treacherous, Richelle races to unmask the Phantom.

Welcome to Raven Hill. . .where danger means business.

■SCHOLASTIC

APPLE SERIES